Butterfly Wishes

The Wishing Wings

Jennifer Castle
illustrated by Tracy Bishop

BLOOMSBURY
NEW YORK LONDON OXFORD NEW DELHI SYDNEY

First published in the United States of America in December 2017
by Bloomsbury Children's Books
www.bloomsbury.com

Bloomsbury is a registered trademark of Bloomsbury Publishing Plc

For information about permission to reproduce selections from this book, write to
Permissions, Bloomsbury Children's Books, 1385 Broadway, New York, New York 10018
Bloomsbury books may be purchased for business or promotional use. For information on
bulk purchases please contact Macmillan Corporate and Premium Sales Department at
specialmarkets@macmillan.com

Library of Congress Cataloging-in-Publication Data
Names: Castle, Jennifer, author.
Title: The wishing wings / by Jennifer Castle.
Description: New York : Bloomsbury, 2017. | Series: Butterfly wishes ; 1
Summary: Just after sisters Addie and Clara move to the country, they
discover magical butterflies called Wishing Wings that need their help to
lift a dark enchantment.
Identifiers: LCCN 2017007247 (print) | LCCN 2017033801 (e-book)
ISBN 978-1-68119-371-7 (paperback) • ISBN 978-1-68119-491-2 (hardcover)
ISBN 978-1-68119-372-4 (e-book)
Subjects: | CYAC: Butterflies—Fiction. | Wishes—Fiction. | Magic—Fiction. |
Sisters—Fiction. | Moving, Household—Fiction.
Classification: LCC PZ7.C268732 Wis 2017 (print) | LCC PZ7.C268732 (e-book)
DDC [Fic]—dc23
LC record available at https://lccn.loc.gov/2017007247

Typeset by Westchester Publishing Services
Printed and bound in the U.S.A. by Berryville Graphics Inc., Berryville, Virginia
2 4 6 8 10 9 7 5 3 1 (paperback)
2 4 6 8 10 9 7 5 3 1 (hardcover)

All papers used by Bloomsbury Publishing, Inc., are natural, recyclable products
made from wood grown in well-managed forests. The manufacturing processes
conform to the environmental regulations of the country of origin.

The Butterfly Wishes series

The Wishing Wings

Tiger Streak's Tale

Coming soon

Blue Rain's Adventure

Spring Shine Sparkles

For S. and C.,
the butterfly spirits in my life

The Wishing Wings

PROLOGUE

The sun scattered gleaming streaks of light through a grove of willow trees. Two butterflies flitted in and out of the rays, riding the breeze toward one tree that was taller and thicker than the others.

In the center of this tree was a deep hollow covered with a carpet of shaggy moss. The butterflies landed softly on it.

"Do you see, Mama?" said one butterfly as she climbed to the top of the hollow. In a neat row hung four gray shapes. Each one was a chrysalis, a small, hard bubble inside which a caterpillar was changing into a butterfly. "The chrysalides should be gold," added the butterfly, "but they're not!"

This butterfly's wings were colored pink and turquoise, with cloud-shaped patterns on them. Now she flapped those wings nervously, hovering around the four chrysalides.

"Yes, Sky Dance," the other butterfly said with an echo of worry. "I do see. They should be lighting up, too." She was bigger, splashed with shades of brilliant red, forest green, and shining silver. The colors made a pattern that looked like a rose on each wing. She was Queen Rose Glow.

Sky Dance landed next to her mother. "Something's very wrong," she said, her voice shaking.

"I feel it, too," murmured Rose Glow. "These New Blooms are surely under a dark enchantment. Who knows what they'll be like when they emerge? If they can't grant someone a wish by sunset on their first day . . ."

". . . they'll lose their magic," finished Sky Dance. The thought of it made her shudder.

One chrysalis was wiggling a bit. Almost dancing. Mother and daughter stared at it with extra love and excitement in their eyes. It was special to them.

"Your sister will have her new wings before the sun breaks over that hill," said Rose Glow.

"I can't wait to see her!" Sky Dance exclaimed, but then she got serious again. "But, Mama," she added, "who would put such a curse on the New Blooms?"

Rose Glow's huge eyes grew darker. "Someone who wants to steal their magic for themselves," she said. "If the New Blooms lose their magic, we all lose a little magic, too. Our magic might even get so weak that it disappears completely." Rose Glow touched a wing to one of Sky Dance's wings and added, "The time has come for you to seek help on the far side of the meadow."

Sky Dance knew what that meant. It frightened her, but she didn't let it show.

The chrysalis shook harder. As it began to slowly split open, both butterflies took a breath and filled their hearts with hope.

CHAPTER ONE

Addie Gibson lay on the floor of her new bedroom, surrounded by boxes. She rested her head on one labeled Books, which was not at all comfortable, but it felt good to take a break from unpacking.

She stared out the window, where all she could see was blue sky and the corner of one puffy cloud. *What is Violet doing right now?* Addie wondered, running her fingers over the woven bracelet on her wrist and thinking of her best friend. *Does the sky look the same out her window?* It had only been three days since Addie's family moved from the city to Brook Forest, but she already missed Violet so much that it hurt.

Suddenly, the bedroom door burst open and there stood Clara, Addie's younger sister. She clutched a stuffed orange cat under one arm.

"I can't find my pencils and sketch pads," Clara announced angrily. "Do you have them?"

"I don't know," replied Addie. "I just opened a box of art supplies. Look over

there." She pointed to a big box in the corner.

Clara marched over to the box and looked inside, then pulled out a set of colored pencils. "Aha! You *did* take them!"

"I did not!" Addie snapped back. "The movers must have packed up our stuff together."

Addie heard the jingle of a collar. Her little black-and-white dog, Pepper, scurried into the room and jumped into Addie's arms.

Clara looked at Addie and the dog with a frown. She asked, "Why does Pepper always take your side? He likes you better, and it's not fair. I've been begging Mom and Dad for my own dog for ages!"

The girls' mother appeared in the doorway behind Clara and clapped her hands. "Both of you, hush," she commanded. "You haven't stopped fighting since we first walked into this house!"

Clara gave her mother a furious look, then gave Addie a *super* furious look, and stomped off. They heard her bedroom door slam.

Mom sighed, then said to Addie, "Forgive your sister. She's really sad about the move."

"She must be," added Addie, "if she's walking around hugging Squish." Squish was the name of Clara's stuffed cat, her favorite toy since she was a baby.

Mom nodded. "Brook Forest is so different from the city. I know it's a big change. Are you sad, too?"

Addie buried her face in the scruff of Pepper's neck. "I'm okay," she said. It wasn't completely true. She *was* sad, but she was trying hard not to be.

"Everything will be better once we're settled in," Mom reassured her. "It won't seem so different anymore, and you'll both make new friends. Why don't you take Pepper outside while I help your sister calm down?"

"Outside?" asked Addie.

Her mother laughed. "Yes, honey. We have a backyard now. You should be exploring it."

"But there's nature out there! Dirt and leaves and bugs and . . . flying things."

"Isn't it wonderful?" Mom said with a smile. "Catch one of them, then bring it back for us to see."

❦ ❦ ❦

Pepper tugged hard at his leash, pulling Addie from the house onto the back deck, and then onto the grass.

"Okay, okay!" she grumbled at her dog. "I get it! You like it out here. That makes one of us."

Truth was, Addie *did* like her yard. She just didn't like the woods that lay beyond it. The stretch of grass behind the house ended at a line of identical trees that made a kind of fence. All Addie could see on the other side of them were more trees, branches, and leaves. It was as if they went on forever. She could hear strange noises, too. Her parents said it was only birds chirping and squirrels scampering, just like in the park near their old apartment, but here they sounded extra-spooky.

Suddenly, there were giggling voices nearby. Addie peered across some bushes to the house next door and glimpsed the top of a swing set. Maybe she would meet the neighbor kids soon. The thought of it made her stomach do a flip-flop.

The kids started shouting at one another, and Addie tried to hear what they were saying. She was listening so hard, she didn't realize she'd loosened her grip on Pepper's leash . . .

Just like that, Pepper was off running, chasing a squirrel toward the row of trees.

"No!" yelled Addie after him, but he shot like a rocket past the trees and into the woods, disappearing almost instantly. "Pepper!" she yelled. "Come back!"

Addie was quiet for a moment, listening for signs of her dog. Out of the corner of her eye, something bright flitted in the distance. When she turned to look, it was gone.

"Pepper!" Addie hollered. "You bad, bad boy!"

There was no time to get help. Pepper was fast. The longer Addie waited to go after him, the farther away he might get.

"Be brave," she said to herself, and took the longest, deepest, courage-creating breath she could.

Addie stepped through the trees, then paused. *This isn't so bad*, she thought. Just a little cooler and darker. Only a little scary.

She took another step, then another. By the third step, she was officially in the woods now . . . and she felt okay!

Addie started running, calling Pepper's name. Somewhere nearby, she could hear the faint jingle of his collar. Her sneakers kicked rocks as she ran, and leaves scratched her bare legs. She ducked under a low branch to avoid smashing into it, but lost her balance and tripped on a thick tree root. Addie barely had time to put out her hands to break her fall.

"Ouch!" she cried as she hit the dirt. She lay there for a second, then slowly stood up, examining her arms and legs to see if she was hurt.

She wasn't, but now she was definitely lost. She brushed herself off, then turned in a circle to see if she could spot a house somewhere. Nothing. There were just woods, woods, and more woods.

"Pepper!" she yelled. "Mom! Clara!"

Nobody answered.

Addie sat down on the ground and hugged her knees to her chest. "You're not scared," she said aloud to herself. "You're fine. Your house is probably on the other side of those trees."

Suddenly, something fluttered past her. Addie saw flashes of pink and turquoise.

Then Pepper emerged from a bush, chasing after it.

🦋 🦋 🦋

Addie followed Pepper's little white-tipped tail into a clearing.

"Pepper, stop!" she commanded. "Leave that butterfly alone!"

Suddenly, the butterfly slowed down, flitting in circles above Pepper's head.

Pepper started running in circles, too. It gave Addie a chance to catch up to him and grab the leash.

"Got you!" she exclaimed once she had it firmly in her hands.

That was strange, Addie thought. It was almost as if the butterfly had done that on purpose, to help her.

Pepper barked at the butterfly, who was still hovering close to them. It darted up and down, back and forth. Addie didn't want Pepper to hurt it.

"Best to tie you up so I can chase this poor thing away," Addie told the dog. She looped his leash around the trunk of a small tree. Once Pepper realized he wasn't going anywhere, he lay down in the grass and put his chin on his paws, panting.

Then Addie turned to the butterfly. "That stinker won't bother you anymore," she said. "Go! Be free!"

But the butterfly didn't leave. It flew even lower. Addie could hear its wings flapping. She could feel the little breeze it made as it flitted by her head. What was it doing?

Maybe it wants to play, thought Addie for a second. But no, that would be ridiculous. Right?

Still, the butterfly did seem very interested in her. Addie was also very interested in *it*. Now that she could get a better look, Addie thought it was the most beautiful and unusual butterfly she'd ever seen. The colors on its wings were so bright, and the pattern on them almost looked like clouds. How strange!

She remembered what her mother said about exploring and catching something. Before she knew it, Addie was reaching out her hands toward the butterfly. It floated above them as if making up its mind, then landed gently, with a tiny tickle, on one of Addie's palms.

Addie carefully cupped her other palm over the butterfly and peered into the little house she'd made with her hands. She'd never been this close to one before. The butterfly slowly flapped its wings, maybe tired out from all that flying. Its antennae stood straight at attention, and it appeared to be looking right back at her with a furry pink face and dark, bead-shaped eyes.

"Hello there," said Addie.

"Hello to you, too," said the butterfly in a voice as high and clear as bells ringing.

Addie was so surprised, she stumbled backward into the dirt again.

CHAPTER TWO

Addie sat up and looked around for the person who'd said hello to her. Nobody was there except for Pepper, who was already snoozing in the sun.

"Who said that?" Addie called out.

The butterfly had escaped Addie's hands when she fell. Now it was zigzagging around her. After a moment, it landed daintily on her knee and said, in that same musical voice, "I did!"

Addie stared at it and blinked twice. Was she imagining this? Had she hit her head?

"You're a butterfly," said Addie. "Butterflies don't talk."

"I'm a Wishing Wing," replied the butterfly matter-of-factly. "And Wishing Wings *do* talk. When we have something to say, of course. We don't go around chattering for no reason. My name's Sky Dance, and I need your help!"

"I'm Addie." Addie was still not sure this was really happening. "What's a Wishing Wing?"

Sky Dance's wings quivered. "We don't have much time," she said anxiously, "but I suppose I should explain a few things first." She was silent for a few moments, her little head tilted as if she were thinking. "Okay," the butterfly continued. "Have you ever suddenly felt like you wanted to take off running because you were so happy? Have you ever started dancing and singing for no reason?"

Addie thought about that. "Yes," she replied. "Not lately, but yes."

"Have you ever felt really strong, like you could do anything you put your mind to?"

"Sometimes," muttered Addie. It had been a while in that department, too.

"That's because of us!" exclaimed Sky Dance, shooting into the air and flying around Addie's head. "That's the power of the Wishing Wing butterflies! Regular butterflies spread pollen. We spread the butterfly spirit . . . by granting wishes. We're magic!"

"Magic . . ." Addie echoed. It was one of her favorite words. "I love magic. Too bad this is just a dream."

"You're not dreaming!" Sky Dance said in a frustrated voice. She landed on Addie's other knee and moved her wings in quick, short flaps. "I'll prove it to you."

"How?"

"By granting you a wish, silly!" Sky Dance suddenly lowered her voice, more serious now. "But you get just one. Every human child gets one. There's only so much magic to go around, you know, so you must choose carefully. What is the thing you want most in the world right now?"

Addie thought about the question. It was a tough one! Nobody had ever asked her that before. She knew she was supposed to name something like a pony or a trillion dollars. But when she closed her eyes and concentrated on what would make her happiest at that moment, the first image that popped into her head was Violet's face. Addie found herself reaching for the bracelet on her wrist— the one that Violet had made for her as a good-bye gift.

Before she knew it, Addie was saying, "I wish my best friend Violet and I could stay close forever, even though we live far apart now."

Sky Dance flitted over to Addie's wrist and examined the bracelet. "Violet must be special to you," she said.

"She is. Missing her is the worst thing about moving to Brook Forest."

"Okay, then!" proclaimed Sky Dance. "I can fix that. Hold out your arm."

Addie did as she was told. Sky Dance paused for a moment, then flew a quick circle around Addie's wrist. She left a trail of colors behind her, a striped rainbow with the dazzling pink, turquoise, and white of her wings.

She flew a second time around Addie's wrist . . . and then a third.

When she was done, Sky Dance landed back on Addie's knee. The rainbow she'd made hung in the air, sparkling like fireworks. When it faded, Addie looked at her arm and gasped in surprise.

The woven bracelet had been transformed into a gleaming gold chain. A heart-shaped locket dangled from the center of it.

"Open it!" said Sky Dance, sounding very pleased with herself.

Addie opened the locket. Inside was a picture of her and Violet together, hugging and smiling at the camera. It was a photo Addie's mother had taken at Addie's last birthday party. Addie was suddenly overcome with the feeling that Violet was with her.

"What . . . How did you . . . When . . ." Addie simply could not find words for this situation.

Sky Dance laughed. "That's Wishing Wing magic for you. It's powerful stuff! I put some extra in the locket. It'll keep your friendship with Violet strong."

"Whoa," muttered Addie, touching the smooth surface of the locket. It was so shiny, she could see her reflection in it. "I love this. Thank you!"

She reached out to hug Sky Dance, then realized that . . . well . . . she couldn't really hug a butterfly. Instead, she put out her finger and Sky Dance landed on it. Addie brought Sky Dance close to her face, and they stared into each other's eyes.

"I guess seeing is believing," Addie said after a moment. "You *are* real."

"Yes, indeed. So you'll help us?"

"What's the trouble, exactly?"

Sky Dance became very still and sighed. "I'm in charge of four New Blooms. That's what we call a Wishing Wing that's just come out of its chrysalis. You know what a chrysalis is, right?"

Addie nodded. "When a caterpillar's ready to turn into a butterfly, it makes a

little house around itself where it does all the changing." She'd seen pictures of them in books, but never one in real life.

"A New Bloom has to earn its magic," continued Sky Dance, "by granting a wish to a human child before sunset. If the New Bloom can't do that, its magic is gone forever! It loses all its colors and its wings become plain white."

"Oh," said Addie softly. "How sad."

Sky Dance folded up her wings so they looked like a single wing, making her look quite solemn. "My sister is one of these New Blooms," she explained. "Someone cast an enchantment on the four chrysalides, but we don't know who or why they'd want to do this. My sister doesn't even realize she's a butterfly. She's confused and afraid. She has to find a human child who needs a wish granted, but she won't leave the Changing Tree!"

"That sounds bad," said Addie. "But why do you think I can help?"

"You can. I had been following you for a little while, but wasn't sure at first if you could help. Then I saw you overcome your fear of the woods by telling yourself to be brave, and I knew you were the one."

It felt strange to Addie—that Sky Dance believed in her like this—but it was a good strange.

"What can I do?" she asked.

"Come with me to Wishing Wing Grove. It's right over there, on the other side of this meadow." Sky Dance began to speak faster as she got more excited. "I'll show you the chrysalides and the Changing Tree! You can meet my parents, too! Then you can help us find a child who needs a wish!"

It did sound wonderful. Still, like with every time she'd faced something new and unfamiliar, Addie couldn't help feeling the tiniest bit afraid.

"What about Pepper?" asked Addie, looking over at her dog. He was still fast asleep.

"Pepper will be fine," assured Sky Dance. "This is Silk Meadow, the entrance to our world. I'll ask a couple of other Wishing Wings to stand guard over him."

Addie and Sky Dance stared at each other for a moment. Addie realized she was on the brink of something amazing. Butterflies! Magic! An adventure! How could she say no?

"Show me the way," said Addie. Now her voice sounded as excited as Sky Dance's.

"Good answer!" laughed Sky Dance, and she took to the air.

Addie began walking quickly after her. She watched Sky Dance zipping and zooming along the breeze. *It's hard to march after a butterfly*, she thought. *It just doesn't feel right.* Addie picked up her pace. She skipped once. Then twice. Sky Dance seemed to be skipping, too, as she flew, and Addie remembered what Sky Dance had said about the butterfly spirit.

Addie sensed it now, in every part of her. She was not sad or shy or scared anymore. She felt *free.*

When Sky Dance sped up, Addie broke into a run alongside her new friend.

CHAPTER THREE

W hen they reached a thicket of
trees at the far side of the
meadow, Sky Dance landed on a low
branch. Addie caught up with her, then
stopped to catch her breath.

"We're here," said Sky Dance proudly.
"Welcome to Wishing Wing Grove!"

Addie stepped into the shade of the

trees and looked around. She saw rocks covered with bright lime-colored moss. Flowers and cattails dotted the grass. Willow trees dangled their leaves like curtains. A cool mist swirled in the air, and Addie could hear the babbling of a nearby creek.

"It's beautiful," sighed Addie.

Two Wishing Wings landed next to Sky Dance. Sky Dance whispered something to them and they flew off toward the spot where Addie knew Pepper lay, hopefully still sleeping.

"Time to meet my parents," proclaimed Sky Dance. "Follow me!"

Addie walked a step behind Sky Dance as they moved deeper into the grove. The air smelled sweet. *Like juice*, thought Addie, *mixed with candy and Mom's perfume.* She slowly breathed it all in, then out.

"Try not to be nervous," said Sky Dance. "They may be queen and king, but they're just Mama and Papa to me, and they're great."

Addie stopped short. "Queen and king?"

Sky Dance chuckled. "Oops! I forgot to tell you! My family are the rulers of Wishing Wing Grove."

"That makes you . . ."

"A princess?" Sky Dance giggled and lowered her voice to a whisper. "Yes, but I don't like to call myself that. I want to be known for being *me*, not just royalty. Even though I'll be queen someday."

Addie was about to ask Sky Dance how she felt about that, but then they came upon a giant boulder. The boulder was covered in a quilt of dazzling colors so lovely it made Addie gasp. It took her a moment to realize the quilt was not made with fabric but with Wishing Wing butterflies. Dozens and dozens of them! Each one's wings were a different pattern of colors and shapes.

"Sky Dance has returned!" Addie heard a voice shout, and a cheer went up among the butterflies. Sky Dance flitted over to the rock, and the crowd made space for her. She landed in front of two butterflies sitting on a ledge at the very top.

Addie hung back, but Sky Dance called out, "Addie! Come closer!"

Addie stepped up to the rock and bowed her head shyly. How do you greet royal butterflies? It wasn't exactly something she'd thought about before. "It's a pleasure to meet you," she finally said.

"Likewise," said one of the two butterflies, bowing her head in return. Addie admired the rose patterns on her red, green, and silver wings. "I am Queen Rose Glow, and we're so happy you've come. We've all been meeting to discuss the enchantment and what it might mean."

"They call me King Flit Flash," said the other butterfly in a low, wise-sounding voice. The king's wings were deep blue and jet black, with white lightning bolts on them. "It's a Wishing Wing's job to help humans, but I've always known that someday we might be the ones who need help. You must be very special if Sky Dance has chosen you."

"Thank you," said Addie, blushing a bit.

"No, thank *you*. How can we ever show our gratitude?" asked Rose Glow.

Flit Flash chuckled. "I have a notion." He whispered something to the queen.

"Excellent idea," she agreed. "Addie will be better able to help us if she can see things the way we see them, even if just for a few minutes." Rose Glow turned back to Addie, who was feel-ing extremely confused . . . and curious. "Addie, have you ever wanted to be a butterfly?"

"Of course!" she burst out. "Who hasn't?"

Sky Dance gasped. "Mama! Are you going to do what I think you're going to do?"

Rose Glow took to the air and hovered over Sky Dance. "Yes. I'd like you to do it with me. You've been studying how, right?"

"Practicing, too!" shouted Sky Dance. She flew up to meet her mother, then turned to Addie. "Stand very still, okay?"

"Okay," said Addie, not sure if she should be excited or nervous. Right then, she was both.

Rose Glow and Sky Dance flew close to each other and touched their wings together. A brilliant rainbow of pink, turquoise, white, red, green, and silver burst from their wings—both butterflies' colors combined. As they flew side by side around Addie, the rainbow wrapped her like a ribbon. They circled once, twice, three times. Then the colors dissolved into a cloud of glitter.

Suddenly, everything looked different.

Addie was no longer gazing down at the rock. She was peering up at it. Sky Dance and Rose Glow landed next to her, but now they looked bigger.

Wait a minute, thought Addie. *I'm the one who changed! I'm BUTTERFLY-SIZE!*

"Stretch out your wings!" instructed Sky Dance.

Addie stretched out what felt like her arms and glanced to her right.

Instead of her arm, there was a wing. She glanced to her left. Another wing. They were magenta and powder blue.

"Oh my gosh!" exclaimed Addie. "My favorite colors!"

"You must be all heart, my girl," said the queen, pointing an antenna at the lavender heart pattern on her wings. "Now the two of you, fly off. This is rare and powerful magic that only two members of the Wishing Wing royal family can make together, but it lasts just a few minutes."

"Come on, Addie!" said Sky Dance. "On the way to the Changing Tree, I'll show you the rest of the grove."

"But I've never flown before!" Addie protested.

"Maybe not like this. But you've imagined it, right? Just imagine it again!"

Addie closed her eyes and thought about all the flying dreams she'd ever had. She flapped her wings like she did in those dreams . . . and was suddenly in the air. It felt as natural as running!

She heard the *flit-flut* of her wings' silk against the breeze as she went higher. The rocks in the grove looked like mountains. The trees looked like skyscrapers. It was weird, but wonderful, to be so weightless. Addie felt all her worries fall far below her to the ground, and she laughed harder than she had in a long time.

Sky Dance flew up beside her and laughed, too. "Now you've really got the butterfly spirit! Follow me!"

They rose above the boulder, then

fluttered farther into the grove. Soon they were looking down on the creek. The water was crystal clear and Addie could see right through to the blue-green of the creek bottom. On the banks, a cluster of bright yellow crickets jumped through the grass.

"We share the grove with them," called Sky Dance. "We keep them safe, and they help us manage the grove. They play great music, too."

Sky Dance led Addie lower to the ground now, until they both landed on the sprawling roots of a huge oak

tree. There was a hole at the base of the tree. A large red ladybug with yellow spots waddled toward it, carrying a basket of leaves on its back.

"The caterpillar nursery's in here," said Sky Dance. "Come on."

Addie followed Sky Dance into the hole. Inside the tree, dozens of caterpillars of various sizes and every possible color crawled around, munching on leaves. More ladybugs with yellow spots rushed around, frantic to feed the caterpillars as they gobbled up whatever was put in front of them.

"They just eat and grow and eat and grow. Being here brings back some good memories," sighed Sky Dance. "When they're ready to spin their chrysalides, the crickets bring them to the Changing Tree."

After they left the nursery, Sky Dance and Addie came upon a long, thin, bright-green caterpillar with tiny red spikes up and down its back.

"Oh!" Sky Dance gasped in surprise. "Hello, Madame Furia."

"Busy day! Busy day!" said Madame Furia sweetly with a giant smile. One of the caterpillar's red eyeballs looked up while the other looked down toward Addie. "I heard about your new friend. Is this her? She makes a stunning butter-fly! Sky Dance,

you're beautiful too, of course. And so brave! The both of you!"

"Thank you," said Sky Dance.

Madame Furia grinned again, even wider. "I must be off! The queen has asked me to interview our cricket companions to see what they know about the enchantment."

They watched Madame Furia inch away in the opposite direction.

Sky Dance asked, "Isn't she nice? It's so sad, what happened to her. She was Mama's best friend, back when they were caterpillars. But she broke the rules of the grove, and as punishment, she wasn't allowed to change into a Wishing Wing. She'll stay a caterpillar forever."

"Wow," said Addie. "What did she do that was so bad?"

"Madame Furia thought another caterpillar was trying to steal Mama away
as a friend, and got jealous. She made it
look like the caterpillar was stealing food
from the others so she'd get in trouble,
but Furia was the one who got caught
in her lies. Mama forgave her. She says
everyone makes mistakes sometimes.
Now she's in charge of the crickets."

Addie was about to ask Sky Dance to
tell her more about these "rules of the
grove," but she started to feel a strange,
tingly feeling in her arms . . . or rather, her
wings. The rainbow suddenly reappeared,
spinning around her. Before Addie knew
it, she was human-size again. She checked
her body, which seemed so big and heavy
now, but everything looked in order.

Sky Dance flitted into her field of

vision. "I guess the magic really does only last a few minutes. How do you feel?"

"Like myself. A little sad not to be a butterfly anymore."

"Well, maybe it won't be the last time," said Sky Dance. "Look, we're here at the Changing Tree."

It was an enormous willow, with a thick trunk and branches that curved in all directions. The leaves looked green at first, but when the wind swished and moved them, they turned purple.

Sky Dance flew up to a hollow in the center of the tree's trunk. Addie drew nearer and took a good look at the chrysalides, which instantly filled her with a sense of sadness and that something was very wrong. They hung gray and still as stones. She counted three. The fourth was just an empty shell, crumpled like a gum wrapper.

"I see what you mean," said Addie. "I'm not a Wishing Wing, but even I can feel the dark magic here. But who? And why?"

"We don't know," replied Sky Dance. "One New Bloom will come out each day. My sister was the first. If we can make sure all four of them grant their wishes in time, maybe then the enchantment will be broken and we can figure out who's behind it all."

"Who's down there?" shouted a high, terrified voice from above. "Whoever it is, go away!"

Addie looked up to a nearby branch of the Changing Tree. There sat a butterfly with wings of purple, peach, and mint green, with leaf patterns on them. The wings glistened in the sun because they were not quite dry.

Sky Dance stared up at this butterfly and her eyes glistened, too, but with tears.

"And that," said Sky Dance softly, her voice quivering, "is my sister Shimmer Leaf."

CHAPTER FOUR

From the tips of her antennae to the bottom edges of her wings, Shimmer Leaf's entire body was shaking with fear.

Addie hated being frightened, but not as much as she hated seeing other creatures scared. She put on a big, warm smile and tried to make her voice as soft and soothing as possible. "Hi, Shimmer Leaf. I'm Addie."

Shimmer Leaf peered down at her, then jumped back and squealed. "You're huge!" she cried. "You're a monster!"

Addie tried not to take that personally. She kept smiling. "I'm just human. I'm also a friend, who's here to help you."

"Don't come near me!" wailed Shimmer Leaf, who then flew to the highest branch of the Changing Tree.

Sky Dance flitted over to Addie's shoulder. "Let me try," she said to Addie, then looked up at Shimmer Leaf. "Shimmer," she cooed. "We went over this earlier. Don't you remember me? I used to come to the caterpillar nursery to sing you songs and read you stories. I'm your big sister!"

"What's a caterpillar?" asked Shimmer

Leaf with a trembling voice. "What's a sister?"

"See what I mean?" said Sky Dance. She sounded like she was about to cry. "We just don't know what to do."

Addie stared long and hard at Shimmer Leaf, filled with sympathy for the butterfly. She wanted so badly to help her, but she'd never seen herself as a saving-the-day kind of girl.

It can't be fun, she thought, *to have no idea who you are, or where you are, or WHY you are.* As she was thinking, her fingers absentmindedly found the bracelet on her wrist. The feel of the smooth, gold chain, and the memory of how wonderful it felt to have a wish come true, sparked an idea.

"Can you tell me more about this 'first

wish' thing?" she asked Sky Dance. "You said she has to find a human child who needs a wish granted. Does she have to find the child herself, or can the child find her?"

Sky Dance thought for a moment. "I don't think it matters. They just have to come together."

A picture was forming in Addie's head, getting clearer by the second. It was a picture of her sister, Clara, as she had watched Addie with Pepper that morning. Clara's face, filled with jealousy, sadness, and loneliness. The face of someone who could really, really use a wish.

"I know what we have to do," said Addie to Sky Dance. "Now it's time to show you *my* home."

🦋 🦋 🦋

As Addie and Sky Dance crossed Silk Meadow, Addie grew anxious about Pepper. She scanned the distance but didn't see him in the spot where she'd left him. If he'd gotten away, she'd have to choose between searching for him and getting Clara to Wishing Wing Grove. It was a choice she didn't want to make.

Suddenly, two little black triangles poked up from the grass. Pepper's ears! Addie laughed with relief.

When she and Sky Dance drew closer, the two butterflies who were standing guard flew to meet them.

"No problems here," said one. "He's kind of sweet and harmless, as dogs go."

"I still don't like them," said the other. "It's that breath. Ugh!"

Addie laughed again, and when Pepper

heard her, he jumped up and started barking.

"Yes, yes. Good boy!" she said as she ran to him and started rubbing his neck. Sky Dance thanked her friends and they headed back toward Wishing Wing Grove.

After she unhooked Pepper's leash from the tree, Addie paused, trying to figure out which way to go from there. She took a step in a certain direction, and it felt right. She took a few more steps, more confident now. "I'm pretty sure this is the way to my house," Addie told Sky Dance as they started walking. "I guess I did know all along."

"Well, actually, you didn't," said Sky Dance with a giggle. "But you do now, because *I* know." When Addie turned to give her a confused look, Sky Dance flew in a little circle. "Yep. Because I granted you a wish, I'm officially your Wishing Wing. We're connected forever. If we're not too far away from each other, I can send you thoughts and you can send them back!"

"A magic butterfly hotline!" Addie exclaimed.

"Exactly! I can't give you any more wishes, but I can help you in other ways, when you need it."

Something bright and fast in the distance caught Addie's eye. It flitted in and out of the trees. It took Addie a few moments to realize what it was.

A white butterfly.

Addie had always loved these. She'd thought they were just as beautiful as the butterflies who had colors and patterns on their wings, but in a pure and simple way. She felt a tickle on her arm. Sky Dance had landed there to watch the white butterfly too, and Addie was overcome with the worried, nervous thoughts Sky Dance was sending her.

"Oh," said Addie. "That was once a New Bloom, right? It wasn't able to earn its magic and become a Wishing Wing."

Sky Dance nodded sadly. "Mama says that if we can't break the enchantment and the New Blooms lose their magic, all Wishing Wing magic will get weaker. It might even fade forever."

That was too terrible a thought. "I'll do my best to keep that from happening," said Addie. "I promise."

They watched the white butterfly disappear, and then continued walking.

At last, there was the fence of trees, and on the other side of it, the bright yellow wood of Addie's house. Even though it had only been her house for a few days, she was super-glad to see it.

As they crossed into the backyard, Addie told Sky Dance, "Since my mom's home, it's better if Clara comes out here. She won't want to, but I'm an expert at getting her to do things she doesn't want to." She smiled at Sky Dance. "That's part of a big sister's job. You'll find out for yourself soon enough."

Sky Dance landed on the railing of the back deck and said, "I hope so."

Addie put Pepper inside the house, then closed the door and stepped onto the deck again. She found a spot directly underneath Clara's window. It was open, thankfully.

"Clara!" she yelled.

Nothing.

"Hey, Clara!" Addie shouted again.

A few moments passed. Then, a grumpy "What do you want?" came floating down from the open window.

"I have a surprise for you!"

"Nice try. I'm not falling for that trick."

"It's not a trick, cross my heart and pinky promise!"

A pause. "Is it gummy worms?" called Clara.

"Nope. It's better!" replied Addie.

Another pause. "I really don't believe you."

"Look, if you see it and don't think it's

better than gummy worms, I'll give you anything you want from my jewelry box. That's a guarantee."

Now a face appeared in the window, peering down at Addie. Addie hid her hands behind her back and opened her palm. She didn't need to say anything. Sky Dance knew to fly over and land on it.

Clara let out a loud sigh, then her face disappeared. Addie and Sky Dance waited a very long few moments. Was she coming? What would Addie do next if she wasn't coming?

Finally, the back door opened and Clara stepped out, still clutching Squish under one arm.

"I'm here," said Clara. "Show me."

Slowly, Addie brought her hand forward from behind her back. She held up

Sky Dance as if the butterfly were sitting on a pedestal, and resisted the urge to shout "Ta-da!"

Clara's eyes grew wide when she saw Sky Dance, and Addie could see the wonder and delight flickering behind them.

"Is this not the most amazing butterfly you've ever seen?" Addie asked her.

Clara was silent as she stared, stunned, at Sky Dance. Addie kept waiting for her sister to finally smile. But instead, Clara scrunched her face into a frown.

"You always find the good things," she said, pouting.

"Oh, Clara," sighed Addie, and that familiar sisterly tension filled the air between them.

They were quiet for a few moments until a high voice crashed through the silence.

"Hey!" Sky Dance snapped at them. "Not everything is a competition, you know. You're two different people, so it's okay to actually *be* different!"

Clara's jaw dropped open and she took a step back.

"I know," said Addie. "She talks. Also, she has magic. And she needs—*we* need—your help."

Clara shook her head hard. "No way. You *are* tricking me. Stop it!"

Addie whispered to Sky Dance, "Remember how seeing is believing?"

Sky Dance nodded, then took flight, flitting back and forth over the backyard, searching for something. When she landed, Addie knew she was supposed to bring Clara over. She beckoned to her sister, and fortunately her sister followed.

Sky Dance was sitting on an acorn that was lying in the grass.

"Are you watching, Clara?" asked Addie. Clara shrugged.

Sky Dance fluttered up and flew three circles around the acorn, leaving her personal pink, turquoise, and white rainbow ribboning behind her. As the colors dissolved into sparkling dust, Clara and Addie both gasped at what had happened.

The acorn was now a tiny seedling with green leaves, just a few inches high.

"Give it ten or fifteen years," said Sky Dance proudly. "That oak tree will be as tall as your house!"

Clara dropped Squish and sank down onto the grass. "Whoa," was all she said.

"Clara," said Addie, kneeling down across from her. "I've discovered something wonderful. And I want to share it with you. Will you let me?"

Maybe it was the word "wonderful," or maybe it was the word "share," but Clara lit up in a way Addie hadn't seen since before their parents had told them they were moving.

"You said something about needing my help?" asked Clara.

Addie and Sky Dance nodded.

"Count me in."

CHAPTER FIVE

O h. My. Gosh." That was all Clara
could say as she stood at the entrance
to Wishing Wing Grove. Addie laughed.
She couldn't remember the last time she'd
seen her sister at a loss for words.

"I know," Addie told her. "We can take
a tour later, but right now we need to go
straight to the Changing Tree."

On their way from the house, Addie and Sky Dance had told Clara all about Wishing Wings and New Blooms. She'd learned about their magic, the mysterious dark enchantment, and, of course, Shimmer Leaf. Now, as they followed Sky Dance through the grove, Clara kept stumbling, too busy looking around in amazement to watch her step. She'd brought along her purple satin backpack, filled with juice boxes, graham crackers, and, of course, Squish.

"Ever since we moved in, I've been watching the woods out my window," whispered Clara, as she stared at a beautiful black, white, and silver Wishing Wing soaring past them. "I had a feeling there was something special out here, but who knew it would be *magically* special!"

She doesn't know the half of it, thought Addie, but she wasn't ready to tell Clara about how she'd been turned into a butterfly. She liked keeping that to herself, at least for a little while.

As they neared the Changing Tree, Sky Dance flitted close to Addie and asked, "What should we do once we get them together?"

"I'm not sure," Addie said. "I haven't thought that far yet."

"Remember, even though it doesn't matter how they meet, Clara still has to catch Shimmer Leaf, then set her free. It's pretty simple when a New Bloom knows what she's supposed to do, but Shimmer won't be caught so easily."

Addie nodded, hoping that between

her, Clara, and Sky Dance, they'd come up with a plan.

The afternoon sun was lower when they finally arrived, and the slanted light made the Changing Tree glow like a lantern in the shade of the grove.

"Wow," said Clara, putting her hand on the thick bark of the trunk and peering into the hollow to see the three gray chrysalides. "This is really happening."

"Shimmer Leaf's up here," called Sky Dance as she flew into the branches.

Addie pointed to show Clara, but then dropped her arm, suddenly confused.

Shimmer Leaf wasn't there.

Sky Dance fluttered frantically in and out of the other branches, higher and higher, finally squeaking "She's gone!" from the top of the tree.

Gone? Addie hadn't even thought of that possibility. Shimmer Leaf had seemed too afraid to move.

"I saw it all!" cried an excited voice. Addie looked down. At her feet sat something green and red. Madame Furia. Addie lowered her hand and let the caterpillar climb on, then brought her close to her face. Clara came to listen and Sky Dance landed on Addie's arm.

"What did you see?" Addie asked Madame Furia.

"Oh, it was awful," she said, her eyes rolling around in tiny circles. "I was on my way back home when I saw two gigantic blue wasps surround Shimmer Leaf on that branch. They were buzzing so loudly, it hurt my ears! Every time she flew to a new branch, they followed her. She hopped higher and higher and those wasps kept buzz-ing louder and louder! Finally, she had no choice but to fly away from the  tree. The wasps chased her . . . and that was the last I saw of any of them." Madame Furia's entire body trembled, segment by segment. "The poor thing! And your mother and father are going to be so worried!"

"We'll find her," said Sky Dance. "We have *two* human girls helping us now."

Madame Furia's red eyes looked Clara up and down. "So I see," she said. "Thank goodness!"

"Please go tell my parents what's

happening!" Sky Dance urged Madame Furia. "Tell them to send every Wishing Wing to search the woods. We'll find her, and everything's going to be okay."

Addie put Madame Furia back on the ground, and they watched her inch away as fast as she could.

"Do you really believe that?" Addie asked Sky Dance. "That everything will be okay?"

Sky Dance slowly flapped her wings twice, and Addie realized that must be the butterfly version of a shrug.

"What choice do I have?" replied Sky Dance. "You can't have courage without confidence."

As soon as Sky Dance said it, Addie felt that confidence fill her. This thought-connection really came in handy!

"I think we should split up and search in different directions," said Clara as she sipped on a juice box.

"That makes sense," said Sky Dance. "I can cover a lot more ground flying than you can. Clara, you should stay in the grove, because when we do find Shimmer Leaf, we'll need to know where you are. We have to get you together quickly. Addie, can you take Clara and search around here? I'll fly out into the woods and help the other Wishing Wings."

"Where do wasps usually hang out in the grove?" asked Addie. "Maybe we can start there."

"That's the strangest part," replied Sky Dance. "I've never seen wasps in the grove. They have their own realm nearby, but they know they're not welcome here.

Coming in and causing trouble would break the Great Wasp–Butterfly Peace Treaty created by my grandmother and the old Wasp Queen. That queen died a little while ago. They have a new one now."

Hmmm, thought Addie. Maybe the wasps were not a random coincidence, but rather, part of some bigger problem. Well, they didn't have time to figure it out. The only thing that mattered right then was finding Shimmer Leaf. The sun was sinking lower every minute.

A cluster of other Wishing Wings zoomed through the air above, and Sky Dance rose up to join them. Addie and Clara waved goodbye as they watched the patchwork of brilliant, fluttering colors disappear into the distance. Addie sent her strongest *Good luck!* thoughts to her butterfly friend.

"So," said Clara as she stuffed her empty juice box into her backpack, then grabbed Squish and tucked him under one arm. "Where do we look first?"

Addie led Clara as they backtracked through Addie's flight as a butterfly, starting with the caterpillar nursery, then the creek, then the stretch of boulders where she'd first met Sky Dance's royal parents. Clara kept pausing to touch every surface she could—moss, grass, water, bark, leaves, rock—and let out a bewildered "Ooooh" each time.

Again and again the sisters called, "Shimmer Leaf!" pausing to listen for buzzing wasps or a high, trembling voice. They stood at the base of every tree and peered up, scanning the branches and leaves for flashes of Shimmer Leaf's purple, peach, and mint-green wings. Addie and Clara climbed onto each large rock to get just a little closer to the sky, watching for the smallest movement anywhere.

"This is pointless," said Addie after a while, collapsing onto a rock. "We're

stuck here on the ground. How can we find a butterfly who may have flown far away and could be fifty feet high in a tree?"

"It would be worse if we were just sitting around, doing nothing," said Clara as she hopped from one boulder to the next.

"I guess you're right," agreed Addie.

Clara paused and spun around. "Wait! You're saying I'm right?"

"Oh, be quiet. It's not the first time I've ever said you were right."

"It sure feels like it," Clara huffed.

Addie stood up to move away from her sister. She was annoyed now. Why couldn't they get along, even in an enchanted grove? As she took a step onto the next rock, she heard a noise. It was faint, and strange, and very sad.

"Clara, did you hear that?" whispered Addie.

She pointed down. Clara made her way to Addie's rock and they listened again. Clara's face lit up.

"I did! It sounded like something crying."

"It sounded like *Shimmer Leaf* crying!" exclaimed Addie, and without thinking, she held up her hand to Clara. Clara slapped her high-five, and they both shouted, "YES!"

Then another, very different noise rose up from the calm. This noise was angry and threatening. It grew louder and louder. Both girls turned in the direction it was coming from.

Two blazingly blue wasps—each one twice as big as any wasp Addie had ever seen—were flying straight toward them at top speed.

CHAPTER SIX

D uck!" yelled Addie. She jumped
down behind the boulder, pulling
Clara with her.

The wasps raced past like fighter
jets, making almost as much noise. Addie
could hear one of them laugh wickedly as
it went over their heads.

Why did it have to be wasps? When Addie was five, she'd stepped on a small one and it stung her foot. She still remembered how much that hurt and couldn't imagine what a sting from these much bigger bugs would feel like.

"Are they gone?" asked Clara after the buzzing faded, but as soon as she did, the buzzing grew louder again. Both girls stuck their heads up. The wasps were circling back! The girls crouched down again, and Addie grabbed a nearby stick to fight them off. But the wasps didn't attack. They landed on a rock, both of them laughing hard.

"That was great!" shouted one, who sounded female. "We haven't had the chance to scare a human kid in a long time!"

"Look at them down there," said the other. This one sounded like a boy. "They're curled up like little snails! They won't get in our way."

"Hey, humans!" taunted the first wasp. "Thanks for helping us find the New Bloom!"

Addie winced. It had never occurred to her that the wasps might be watching them search for Shimmer Leaf.

"So, Poke," said the boy wasp. "What next?"

Addie could see the wasps through a gap between two rocks. She watched the girl wasp fly down to the spot where they'd heard Shimmer Leaf's sobs.

"You were right, Striker. She's definitely in some kind of crevice, where these two rocks come together," Poke said. "But it's a really small opening. We can't squeeze in there to get her."

"Ha!" laughed Striker. "I never thought being big would be a problem!" He flew down to land next to Poke. "Can't we just keep her here until sunset, when her magic disappears?"

"Don't be dumb," sneered Poke. "We have specific orders to chase her back to the Wasp Realm."

Addie and Clara looked at each other with alarm.

"We can't let that happen," whispered Clara.

"But if we run to get help, they'll come after us . . ." Addie whispered back, but then she realized something important. "Wait a minute! I don't have to *run*! I can *think*!"

Addie had forgotten to send Sky Dance a message that they'd found Shimmer Leaf. She knew she just had to think the words WE FOUND HER! PLEASE HELP US! COME QUICK! as hard as she could, and Sky Dance would hear her.

"If only we could distract the wasps," said Addie.

"Or maybe we could trick them some-how," added Clara.

Clara's suggestion set off an idea in Addie's head. For a minute or so, every-thing was eerily quiet and tense as the wasps paced in front of the crevice and

Addie focused on her idea. Then she heard a *flit-flut* near her ear and turned to see Sky Dance sitting on her shoulder.

Addie opened her mouth to say something, but Sky Dance whispered, "Shhh! We don't want them to know she's here."

"Who?" asked Addie softly.

"My mom. The queen." Sky Dance pointed an antenna at Addie's knee, where Queen Rose Glow was now landing, looking very sad.

"Oh," sighed Queen Rose Glow. "I can hear Shimmer Leaf crying. My poor baby!"

"I think I have a plan," said Addie. She then leaned close to Sky Dance's antennae to tell her. When she was done, Sky Dance's eyes lit up.

"Is that even possible?" asked Addie.

"I think so!" replied Sky Dance. She

flew over to her mother and murmured to her. The queen looked at Addie, then nodded excitedly.

Addie turned to Clara. "Something's going to happen. Don't freak out."

Before Clara could say a word, Sky Dance and Rose Glow took flight, touching their wings together to spout the rainbow of their combined colors. As they circled Addie three times, strands of pink, turquoise, white, red, green, and silver filled the air with sparkles.

Clara watched, her jaw hanging open.

When all the glitter faded before Addie's eyes, she didn't bother to examine herself. She knew there was no time for that. Instead, she flapped her newly formed butterfly wings and took off as fast as she could. The ground fell away below her, and the air rushing past felt natural and familiar. It was like she'd always been flying!

She knew that to the stunned Clara, it looked like her sister was gone and in her place was a Wishing Wing butterfly.

She also knew that to the wasps, she looked like Shimmer Leaf. Sky Dance and Rose Glow had used their magic to turn Addie's butterfly wings the same colors as Shimmer Leaf's. The leaf patterns were not there—she understood that patterns were special to each Wishing Wing and couldn't be copied—but she hoped the wasps wouldn't notice.

"Poke!" Addie heard Striker yell. "She's making a break for it!"

"Let's get her!" shouted Poke. "Nice try, butterfly! We're too fast for you!"

Addie felt Sky Dance sending her a thought message. *Head for the two tall pine trees to the south*, it said. *Fly until you turn human again, and we'll take care of the rest.*

As she flew toward the pine trees, Addie could hear the wasps buzzing behind her, but her head start kept them at a distance. This was just like the time she raced a girl named Jillian in gym class at her old school. Jillian usually beat her at everything, but on that day, Addie had sprinted from the word "Go!" and didn't look back until she crossed the finish line first. Addie remembered how proud she'd been to realize she was a faster runner than she'd thought, and that powered her butterfly wings now.

Addie kept flapping as hard as she could and found a breeze, which gave her an extra push. The pine trees were getting closer and closer . . . while the wasps' buzzing grew louder and louder . . .

She'd made it! Addie flew right through the space between the two pine trees.

Then, with a *thump*, she fell backward on the ground. In an instant, she had all of her usual parts and was Addie-size again.

The wasps sped by. The branches of the pine trees had blocked their view and they hadn't seen Addie change into a human. She caught her breath and watched as two bright Wishing Wings, then four, then ten, flew into the gap between the trees. Still more butterflies came, flying so close to one another she couldn't tell where one butterfly's wings ended and another's began. The flickering colors looked like a giant kaleidoscope.

They were filling the gap between the pine trees. *A net!* Addie realized.

Suddenly, Queen Rose Glow flew up to her.

"Are you all right, my dear?" she asked.

"Yes, I'm fine!"

"Run back to Sky Dance and your sister! We'll hold the wasps back with some group magic."

Addie nodded, jumped up, dusted herself off, and raced back to the rocks.

When she got there, she found Clara kneeling on the ground in front of

Shimmer Leaf's hiding place. Sky Dance perched on a rock nearby, staring nervously in the direction of the sun. The bottom tip of it had dropped behind the treetops, and the sky was tinted pink. It wouldn't be long before it was completely gone.

Clara put her face as close as she could to the crevice's opening. Addie could still hear Shimmer Leaf's sobs coming from inside.

"Shimmer Leaf," Clara said softly to the butterfly. "I understand that you're scared. I understand that you're lonely. I know exactly how that feels, because I just found myself in a brand-new place, too."

Clara paused, and they listened. It was quiet. The sobs had stopped.

"But now I see that I'm not alone at all," continued Clara. "There are friends around me everywhere. Some, I just haven't met yet."

Clara glanced quickly at Addie. Addie smiled back.

Clara took a deep breath and put her face to the crevice once more. "Can I be your first new friend, Shimmer Leaf?"

A tiny, shaking voice said, "Okay."

"Here," said Clara, reaching as much of her hand into the opening as would fit. "Climb on. I'll help you out of there."

Addie held her breath, and she knew Sky Dance was doing the same. They waited for a long moment. Addie glanced up to see that even more of the sun had disappeared, and her heart thudded harder.

Clara pulled her hand out of the crevice and clapped the other one on top. She smiled big. Shimmer Leaf must be inside!

"I've got you," whispered Clara to her hands. "You're safe with me."

"Are you sure?" asked the tiny voice.

Clara opened her palms.

A burst of color shot into the air and fluttered away.

CHAPTER SEVEN

N o!" shouted Clara as they watched Shimmer Leaf dart toward the sky. "Where is she going?"

Sky Dance began chasing her sister, but then paused in midair. Shimmer Leaf was slowing down. She flew in a U-shape and headed back toward them, landing gently on Clara's still-open palm.

"Clara!" said Shimmer Leaf. Her voice didn't sound scared anymore. It rang out bright and happy. "You caught me, then set me free! That means I'm your Wishing Wing!"

Sky Dance rushed to land next to Shimmer Leaf.

"Shimmer Leaf!" she cried. "Do you know who you are?"

Shimmer Leaf touched her wing to Sky Dance's. "Yes, Sky, of course. Why wouldn't I?" She let out a huff and turned back to Clara. "Sisters can be so irritating."

Sky Dance laughed and said, "The enchantment's broken!" She flew two joyful flips in the air.

"Yay!" cheered Addie. "Nice work, Clara!" Then she caught sight of the sun and remembered there was one more, very important thing they still had to do. "Shimmer Leaf! The wish!"

"Oh!" exclaimed Shimmer Leaf, looking at the pink-and-red-striped sky. "Where did the day go?" She turned to Clara. "I'm here to make a wish come true for you."

"Really? That's amazing!" said Clara, pretending she didn't already know it. She winked at Addie and Sky Dance. She'd had a little time to think about her wish, but made a face like she was just deciding now. "You know what I've always wished for? A pet of my very own."

"A pet of your very own . . ." echoed Shimmer Leaf, nodding. "That's a great wish. Let's see, I think I can make that happen."

She looked around, her antennae pointing back and forth. Squish was lying on a nearby rock. Clara must have left him there when she went to coax Shimmer Leaf out of her hiding spot. When Shimmer Leaf spotted him, she shot into the air. In an instant, she was wrapping Squish in her glittering purple, peach, and mint-green rainbow. After her third time around, she landed.

They all watched the sparkles shimmer and blink. Addie couldn't wait to see what would appear in Squish's place! She laced her fingers through Clara's and squeezed her sister's hand.

But when the colors and sparkles vanished, there was nothing there.

No Squish. No real live pet.

"What happened?" Clara burst out, nearly in tears. "Where's Squish?"

Sky Dance and Shimmer Leaf didn't answer. They were both looking at the last tiny bit of sun as it fell behind the treetops. It was officially sunset. Sky Dance turned to her sister and looked her up and down.

"You're still a Wishing Wing!" she remarked. "We did it!"

"You mean, I earned my magic?" asked Shimmer Leaf.

"Yes! Yes! Thanks to Addie and Clara! I'll tell you the whole story later. I have a feeling these girls have to get home right away."

"Where's Squish?" cried Clara.

"That's why you have to get home," replied Shimmer Leaf with a mischievous smile. "Hurry! There's someone there who needs you."

Clara gasped excitedly and grabbed her backpack. "Come on!" she said to Addie.

Addie led her sister a few steps in the direction of Silk Meadow, then suddenly stopped. She turned back to the butterflies.

"When will we see you again?" called Addie.

"If the next chrysalis opens and we have the same problem . . . then very soon, I'm sure," answered Sky Dance. "Maybe even tomorrow! We'll need your help finding children who need wishes."

"We'll be ready!"

"We will?" whispered Clara to her. "We don't know any other kids here."

"We don't know them *yet*," said Addie. "But you said yourself: there are friends everywhere."

Clara grinned. "I did say that, didn't I?" She waved to their first two new friends. "Goodbye, Sky Dance! Goodbye, Shimmer Leaf!"

The butterfly sisters flitted into the air, flapping their wings in their own special kind of wave.

"Let's go!" said Addie. She grabbed Clara's hand again and they raced toward home.

🦋 🦋 🦋

They ran until they reached the border between the woods and their house, then stopped to catch their breath.

"Hey, Addie," said Clara, watching a

bird fly overhead. "That turning-into-a-butterfly thing was pretty crazy. But did you notice how I didn't freak out?"

"Yes, I'm so glad," Addie replied.

"However," said Clara with a serious face now. "I will if I don't get a turn to do that, too!"

Addie couldn't help but laugh. "I understand. Hopefully, there will be a chance next time."

They stepped through the trees that bordered their backyard. It felt strange, yet wonderful, to be back where their adventure had started just a short time ago.

Clara began looking frantically around. "Shimmer Leaf said there was something here that needed us . . ." she said. "But I don't see anything. Do you?"

Addie walked a circle around the yard, but didn't notice anything either.

"She could have given us a hint," said Clara, frustrated. She picked up a log from the woodpile to peek underneath.

"Maybe she didn't think we needed it," said Addie. She thought for a moment, then remembered something. "Hey," she added. "When we were searching for Shimmer Leaf, we found her by listening. Maybe we should do that now."

They were quiet for a few moments. Addie heard the wind whistle through the trees, the neighbors laughing next door, and a car rumbling down the road.

Then, she heard something else:

Mew.

"Addie!" Clara exclaimed.

"I heard it, too!"

"Where is it coming from?"

Mew. Mew, mew.

"I think it's coming from under the deck!" said Addie. They both rushed to the side of the deck, where there was a small space between the wooden boards and the ground. Addie was about to crawl under, but then stopped herself.

This was Clara's wish. It was Clara's discovery, and Clara's moment. She didn't want to take that from her sister.

Addie stepped aside and motioned for Clara to go ahead.

Clara dropped to her knees and disappeared under the deck. A few moments later, she reappeared, scrambling backward with one hand.

In the other, she clutched a tiny, orange-striped kitten. He had big blue eyes just like Squish, and smudges of dirt on his face and paws just like him, too.

Mew, the kitten cried, but he sounded less frightened and lonely now.

Clara stood up and hugged the kitten, kissing his fuzzy little head.

"Squish!" she cooed softly to him.

Addie had never seen her sister so filled with joy. It was like she'd never been sad, or angry, or lonely in her life.

The back door slid open, and Addie's mother and father stepped out.

"Addie, there you are!" exclaimed

Mom. "Have you girls been outside this whole time?"

"Yup," said Addie. It wasn't a lie, after all.

"What's that you've got there?" asked Dad when he noticed the fluff of orange nuzzled under Clara's chin.

"We found a kitten under the deck!" said Clara. "Isn't he the cutest, sweetest thing ever?"

"He looks just like your Squish," remarked Dad.

"He must belong to someone," said Mom.

He belongs to Clara, thought Addie, but she knew she couldn't say that. Instead, she said: "Can we take care of him until we find the owner? If there isn't an owner, can we keep him?"

Mom and Dad looked at Clara. There was no denying it: Clara had never seemed happier. Addie's parents exchanged a long glance, then finally smiled.

"Okay," said Mom. "Let's bring him in and clean him up. The poor thing must be hungry!"

Mom and Dad went inside, and Clara followed. As she passed Addie, Addie could hear Squish—a real live breathing Squish!—purr like a loud motorboat engine. Addie knew that if humans could purr, Clara would be doing it, too.

Before Addie went into the house, she turned to stare at the woods. Now she knew so much about them: There were dangers and dark enchantments out there, but also wonders beyond her imagination. Every New Bloom who needed their help earning its magic would mean another set of challenges.

Addie felt a flutter in her stomach.

She couldn't wait for the next adventure to begin.

TURN THE PAGE FOR A SNEAK PEEK
AT ADDIE AND CLARA'S NEXT
MAGICAL BUTTERFLY ADVENTURE!

AVAILABLE NOW!

"Hello again," said Clara to Shimmer Leaf. "How was your first night as a butterfly?"

Shimmer Leaf stretched out her new wings. They were bright purple, peach, and mint green with leaf patterns. "Once I figured out how to tuck these things in for sleeping," she said, "it was great!"

The two girls and the two butterflies all giggled again, then fell silent . . . and serious.

"You called us," said Addie. "Does that mean . . ."

"Yes," replied Sky Dance. "Another New Bloom came out of her chrysalis this morning."

"It's our cousin Tiger Streak," added Shimmer Leaf.

"Was it just like with Shimmer?" asked Addie. Shimmer Leaf had woken up not knowing who she was, or that she had to grant a wish before sunset. It had taken

lots of quick thinking, plus a dash of courage, for Clara to catch the butterfly and set her free.

"We're not sure," said Sky Dance. "She flew away from the Changing Tree before we could talk to her. But she's been seen throughout the grove."

"You mean *heard* throughout the grove," corrected Shimmer Leaf.

Sky Dance sighed. "That too."

"What do you mean?" asked Clara.

"Apparently," said Sky Dance, "Tiger Streak is fluttering around making a very *un*-butterfly-like noise."

"*Bzzz*," added Shimmer Leaf.

"Like a bee?" asked Addie, frowning.

"Exactly," said Sky Dance.

"That, uh, seems like a bad sign," said Clara.

"*Exactly*," agreed Shimmer Leaf. "Will you help us find her? We'll also need to find a human child to catch her and set her free to break the enchantment. Then Tiger Streak can grant that child a wish and earn her magic."

"We'll do whatever we can," Clara said.

"We're ready," Addie assured them.

Jennifer Castle is the author of the Butterfly Wishes series and many other books for children and teens, including *Famous Friends* and *Together at Midnight*. She lives in New York's Hudson Valley with her husband, two daughters, and two striped cats, at the edge of a deep wood that is most definitely filled with magic—she just hasn't found it yet.

www.jennifercastle.com

Tracy Bishop is the illustrator of the Butterfly Wishes series. She has loved drawing magical creatures like fairies, unicorns, and dragons since she was little and is thrilled to get to draw magical butterflies. She lives in the San Francisco Bay Area with her husband, son, and a hairy dog named Harry.

www.tracybishop.com